Delilah Darling

is in the Library

Jeanne Willis

Illustrated by Rosie Reeve

My name is **Queen Delilah.**

I come from a land far, far away.

Only my mother likes to keep it secret.

She always says,

"But, Delilah, darling, you were born here!"

And,

"No, Delilah.
You cannot wear a crown to school.
You are not
the
Queen."

That is nonsense, I'm afraid.
If you don't believe me,
ask my brother, Smallboy.
Only you won't understand him
because he only speaks
Far Away Language.

And don't ask Daddy
because he's busy.

Now this is **Gigi**. She is my **Old Pear**.
An Old Pear is someone who tries to look
after you until your mother comes home.
She is French, which is a place in France.

Gigi says,
"Come, Delilah, my little **cabbage**.
Let us go to the library."

Oh, good.
I love looking at books.

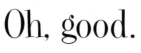

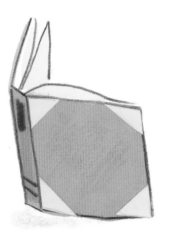

And **smelling** them.

And **shutting** them like this . . .

S^NA P !

when I get
to the end.

The library is full of extremely interesting books:
some have **pictures**,
some have **words**
and this one
has a squashed
baked bean
on
page 5.

But do you know? It's not a bit like the library
in my faraway land.
Where I come from,
they always give you
free
sticky
buns.

Smallboy is hungry, so I ask Gigi,
    "When will they bring the buns?"
And she says,
    "What is buns?
I am not understanding.
    Ask that Library Anne."

So me and Smallboy go
    and ask Library Anne,
but she says,
    "No food in here, please!"

And I say,
"Really?? Where I come from, everyone eats in the library. There is a man who walks round with a big tray and he shouts,

'WHO WANTS A BUN?'"

"Shhh!" says Library Anne.
But everybody says, "Ooh, are there buns?
Are they free? We want buns!"

"Now, that ..." says Library Anne,
"is why we don't shout in the library."

Library Anne says,
"I don't know where you come from,
young lady, but we have
different rules in this library."

I tell her I come
from a land far, far away.

"Well, run along and find
a nice book about it," she says.

So I run along, but Library Anne says,
"No running in
the library, please!"

Which is odd, because where I come from
everyone runs in the library.

Anyway, I try to find
a book about the land
where I come from,
but I can't.

Anyone would think it didn't exist.

Then Smallboy says,
"Try up there!" in Far Away Language.
So I start
to climb.

But Library Anne says,
"Goodness, come down!
That is not how we fetch
a book!"

I say,

"Oh, I'm sorry.
Only I couldn't find the trapeze.
Where I come from, there is a trapeze

to reach the

too-high

books."

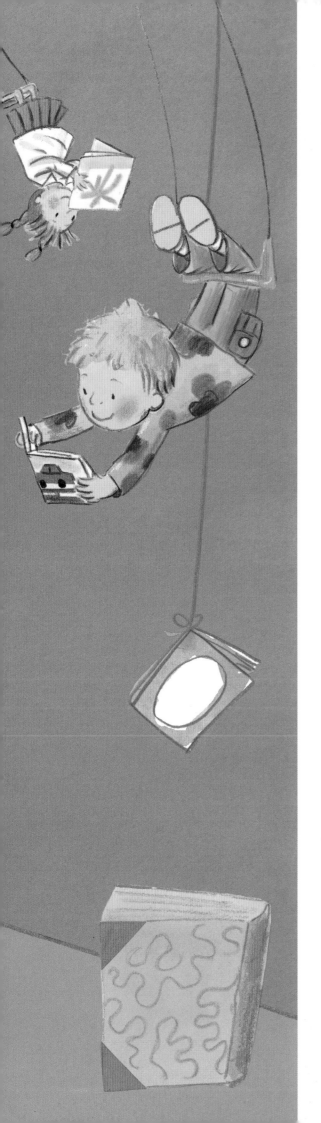

"Hey, I like the trapeze idea," says Mrs Woolly Hat. "I'm short. I never get to read the too-high books."

Library Anne says,
    "There are much more sensible ways of reaching books."

"I will **help** you
find the book
properly."

"Now," she says,
"tell me the **name** of
the **land** where you come from."

Only **I** can't, because
it's **very** hard to say.

Smallboy tells her in Far Away Language
but she doesn't understand.
So I explain that we come from
a tiny little island between
Jafrica
and
Smindia.

Only Library Anne has never heard of such places.

Library Anne opens a big book and says,
"Here is a map of the world.
Can you point to
where you come from?"

But would you **believe** it?
The person who drew the map
forgot to put it on.

Here it is.

A map of the land where I come from.

You can't read its name because it's under my drawing of a Jafrican smelliphant, which is a bit like a Smindian oliphant only smellier.

he ngle

the caves

the camp

the beach

So I give Library Anne
a map I **made** to show her
what the world is **really** like.

Where I come from, we have our own animals,
our own rules and everything.
We even have our own song called
HOORAY FOR QUEEN DELILAH, which I wrote.
"I'd love to hear that!" says Mrs Woolly Hat.

So I stand on a chair and sing it.
Mrs Woolly Hat joins in.

Here are the words so you can sing along too.

Hooray for Queen Delilah,
So beautiful, so brave.
Hurrah for Queen Delilah,
The Kingdom she will save.
Oh, shout hoorah! Oh, shout hooray!
Shout out loud and strong.
Hooray for Queen Delilah,
Who wrote this lovely song!
Tra la!

Library Anne says,
"I wish I lived far, far away.
Please stop singing!"

Then she says,
"Would you like to
borrow a **book**
before you **leave?**"

Where I come from,
we **don't borrow** books
and **leave!**

We all **bring**

our blankets
and bears and a beautiful princess reads to us
until we fall asleep.

"Buns! Blankets! Bears! That's how to run a library," says everyone.

"There are days," says Library Anne, "when I wish I was an astronaut."

"Delilah,
darling,"
says Gigi.

"I think it is time
to say 'Au Revoir'."

We go home.
I tell my mother about the library.
It was **extremely** fun.
And I borrowed a lovely book
called TROPICAL DISEASES.

But it was **nothing like** the library
in the **land** where **I** come from.

"But, Delilah, darling," she says,
"you come from here! We all do."

TROPICAL
DISEASES

TROPICAL
DISEASES

We don't, though.
She's just pretending.
Funny old thing.

"Oh, Mother," I sigh,
"sometimes I think you're living
in a world of your own."

Yes, I know I'm holding my
library book **upside down**.
Where **I** come from,
that's how **everybody** reads.